First published 2020
Text & illustrations copyright Antony Stones
The rights of Antony Stones to be identified
as the author and illustrator of this work
have been asserted.

ISBN 979 867 169 8985

Dedicated to my family,
who always help me
to achieve the
seemingly impossible

Little Rabbit lives on a hill
just at the edge of the wood
and sits watching the flying birds
thinking,

"I wish that I could fly just like them
over the hills and the wood,
over the river and over the town,
oh, how I wish that I could!"

Little Rabbit spoke to Badger,

"I wish that I could fly through the air."

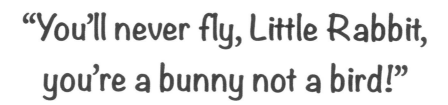

Little Rabbit spoke to Owl,

"I want to fly over the trees."

Little Rabbit spoke to squirrel,

"Why can't I have wings?"

"Because little rabbits have no need for the feathery, flappy things"

Little Rabbit sat on a log,
his ears pulled over his eyes,

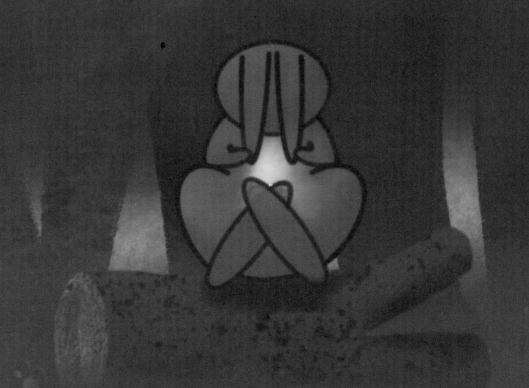

Hedgehog came along and asked,

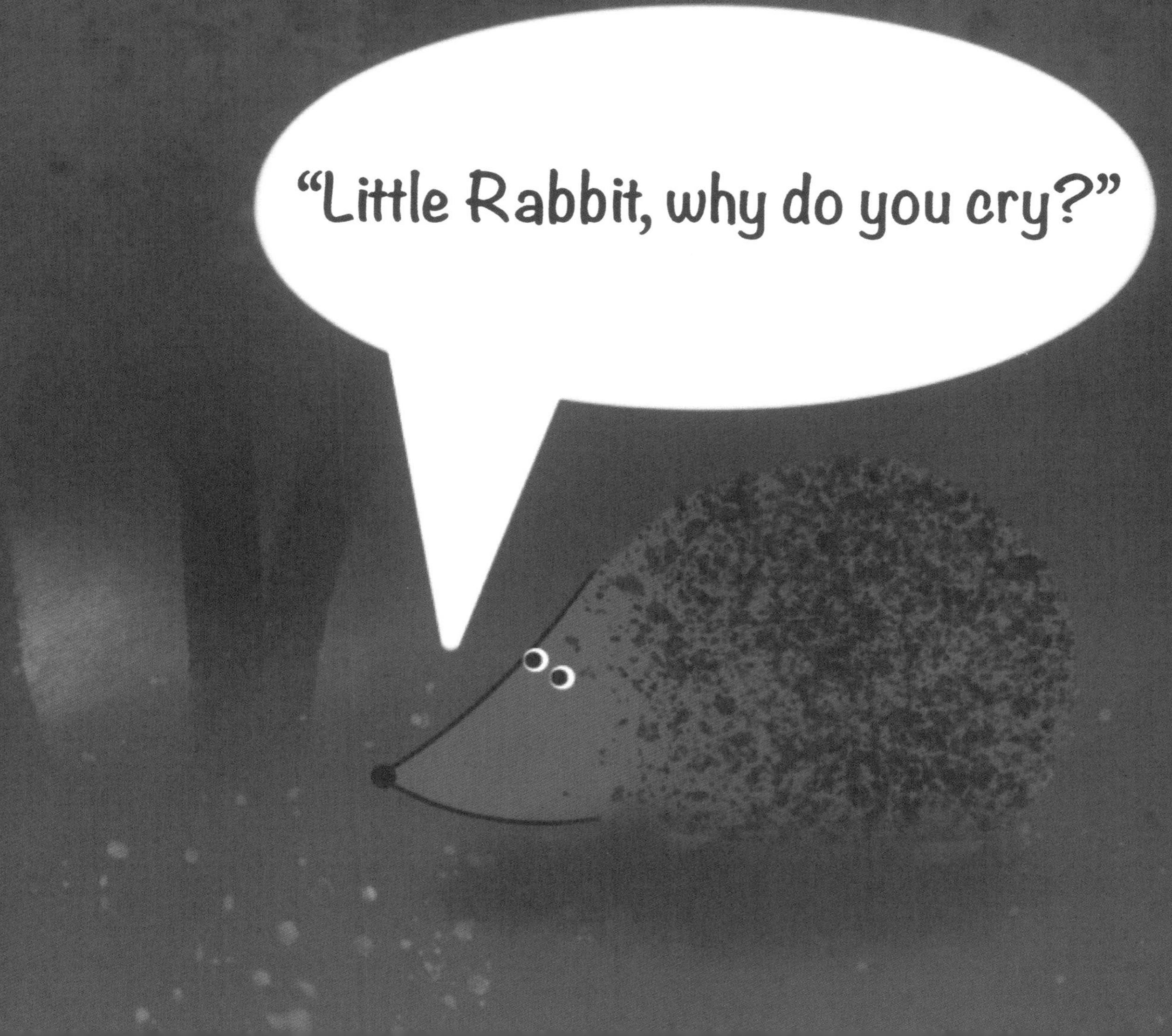

"Because it's silly to want to fly
when you can't if you don't have wings
and because bunnies aren't allowed
feathery, flappy things."

"I don't know if you could ever fly, but I don't know for sure that you can't so I definitely think you should try!"

Hedgehog and Little Rabbit
explored the edge of the woods

looking for sticks and fallen leaves
and gathering all that they could.

They tied the sticks together
and covered them with leaves,

Hedgehog smiled and winked and said,

"You can do anything if you believe!"

Blades of grass were used to strap
the wings to Little Rabbit's back,
with a big deep breath, eyes closed tight,
Little Rabbit ran down the track

Little Rabbit ran and ran,
faster than ever before

until a gust of wind lifted
Little Rabbit off the floor!

Little Rabbit flew into the air
over the hills and the trees,
over the river and over the town
shouting,

"Look at me!"

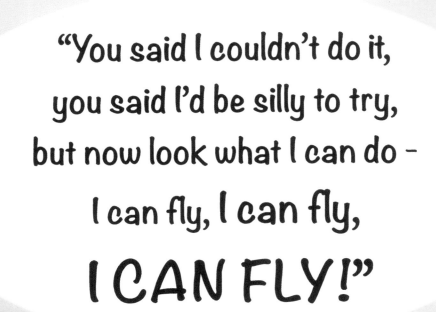

"You said I couldn't do it,
you said I'd be silly to try,
but now look what I can do –
I can fly, I can fly,

I CAN FLY!"

Little Rabbit came back to earth
and gave Hedgehog a great big hug

"You helped me do something amazing,
the first ever Rabbit to fly,
and now it's time that I helped you
so what would you most like to try?"

Hedgehog said,

"This might sound odd
and I know it would be a hassle,
but one thing I've always wanted to do
is play on a bouncy castle!"

THE

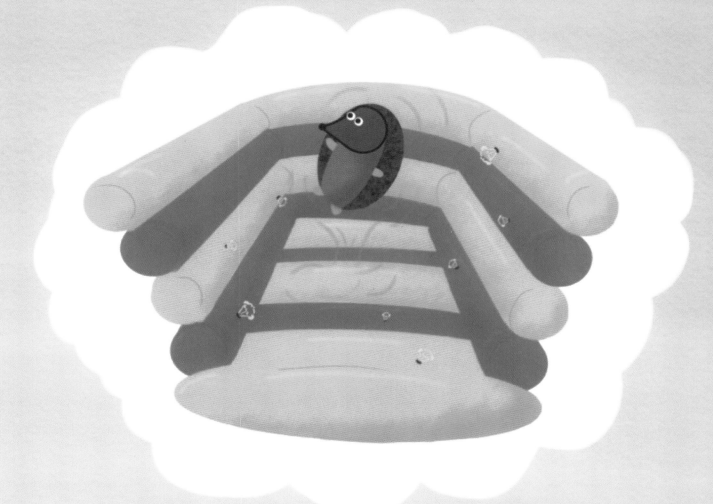

END

From the same author comes this delightful rhyming story of a young puffin looking for love.

Based on the famous puffins of RSPB Bempton, the illustrations beautifully capture their playful, and much-loved, character, helping young children to develop a love for nature and the world around them.

☆☆☆☆☆☆
"My kids loved this book"

Puffin Bill's Extraordinary Week

☆☆☆☆☆
"Beautiful book,
a wonderful read"

☆☆☆☆☆
"Gorgeous, gorgeous,
gorgeous"

written & illustrated
by Antony Stones

☆☆☆☆☆
"This beautifully illustrated
book is a must"

Printed in Great Britain
by Amazon